A FUN & FROLIC BOOK

ISABEL'S NOEL

ISABEL'S NOEL

story by
JANE YOLEN

illustrations by
ARNOLD ROTH

FUNK & WAGNALLS · NEW YORK

For F. K., who has
a special kind of magic

Fifty-four nights ago it had been Halloween.

And tomorrow was Christmas.

Isabel looked at her calendar. There was no mistake. Christmas always came fifty-five nights after Halloween, rain or shine. Every witch knew that.

And Isabel was a witch.

One night to go and she had no present for her mother or her grandmother. Not one bad thing at all.

She had tried black magic. She had tried white magic. She had even tried gray. But they had not worked at all. Isabel was out of ideas and she still had nothing bad for her mother and grandmother.

And tomorrow was Christmas.

Sadly, Isabel walked through the wall. Her black cat Nuncle trailed behind. Isabel knew what *she* would get for Christmas —the same thing she got every year. A new charm for her bracelet brewed especially for the occasion. And a new page for her loose-leaf speller. She was up to G, for "Goodness, removal of."

Her mother and grandmother never had any problem deciding what to give her. *Their* magic always worked. The problem, as usual, was Isabel's. If only she were a good witch—that is, a bad witch—she could have solved it at once with magic. But Isabel wasn't. She didn't even look like a witch. Her eyes twinkled a merry blue. Her hair turned up at the ends. And so did the brim of her hat. And her cat—well, Nuncle was still really more of a kitten.

"What shall I do?" said Isabel as she sat down on the wall of the wishing well by the edge of the woods. Nuncle jumped up on the wall next to her and knocked a pebble into the water. The sound of the splash gave Isabel an idea.

"If witching won't work," she said, "perhaps wishing will."

She reached into her pocket but could find only one coin. "It's my very last bad penny," she whispered to Nuncle. "I'd better save it for a sunny day."

Isabel sighed. "Without a coin, the wishing well won't work. So wishing is out. And witching won't work. We both know what I have to do. It's the only way left."

A cold wind swept through the clearing.

Nuncle shivered.

Isabel looked around. She had to be certain that her mother and grandmother were not watching. They would never let her do such a terrible thing. Imagine—a witch writing to Santa Claus!

No one was near.

Isabel took her wand out of her pocket and cleared a place by the well with her foot. With the tip of the stick she wrote in the sand:

> *Dearest Santa,*
> *Hope you're well,*
> *I need help.*
> *Love, Isabel.*

Her letters were a little wobbly, but correct.

Then Isabel closed her eyes, waved her wand, and spoke her
magic spell:

> *Letters in the sand,*
> *Go forth.*
> *Seek out Santa*
> *In the north.*

She opened an eye and watched. One by one, the letters in the
sand disappeared, smoothed out by an invisible hand.

"I hope it works," Isabel whispered. She wasn't sure it would. She was very poor at spelling.

A loud clap of thunder shook the air. The trees moaned. Suddenly the clearing was filled with smoke.

"Isabel," screeched her mother from the house, "what have you done this time?"

"Oh dear, oh dear," said Isabel, "I've ruined another one. I've just got to remember not to peek or speak before the spell is done."

She ran to the house. The smoke was coming from inside where Grandma was brewing dinner. The door opened itself and Isabel ran in.

There in the middle of her grandmother's cauldron, up to his nose in lizard soup, was a roly-poly stranger in a very wet red suit.

"Ho, ho, ho," said the stranger. Only, because his mouth was filled with soup, it came out "Hrrro, hrrro, hrrro."

"Isabel," screeched her mother, "what have you done and who is this?"

Isabel put her hand to her mouth. "I think," she said very quietly, "I think it's Santa Claus."

Her mother's hair stood up on end.

"Sandy who?" asked Grandma, who was slightly hard of hearing. "Sandy or dirty, it doesn't matter. I don't think he'll help the soup." She tried to stir the cauldron.

"What is Santa doing in our house?" screeched Isabel's mother.

"Yes," said Santa Claus, climbing out of the cauldron and sloshing to the floor. "What *am* I doing in a witch's house? One minute I was packing my sleigh with Christmas goodies and . . ."

"Goodies?" screeched Isabel's mother. "Don't say that word."

"I'm terribly sorry," said Santa. "All I know is that suddenly I was standing on the roof of this hut. There was a chimney and," he shrugged, "I slid down."

Isabel looked at her mother. She looked at her grandmother who was tasting the soup. She looked at Santa who was wringing out his hat. "It's all my fault," she said. "I was just trying to find something for you and grandmother for Christmas. I tried to send a letter to the North Pole. But I guess I spelled it backwards."

She turned to Santa. "I'm not very good at spelling yet. I'm only seven going on eight hundred years old. That's awfully young—for a witch."

And Isabel began to cry.

"There, there," said Santa, who could not bear to see any-one cry—even a witch. "There's no problem as long as I can get back to the North Pole in time."

"I can try to send you back," said Isabel with a sniff. "But I can't promise it'll work."

"Just try your best," said Santa, who knew all about little girls.

"Just try your worst," said Grandma, who knew all about little witches.

Isabel closed her eyes and waved her wand. Up and down, up and down. Then she spoke her spell:

> *One, two, one, two,*
> *Alakazam and kalamazoo,*
> *Witchity, watchity, a miss and a hit,*
> *Anyone around my base is it!*

There was a rumble from the rooftop and a loud, gusty plop. Isabel looked up. The ceiling was beginning to sag.

Isabel and her mother and grandmother ran outside. Santa Claus squooshed out after them.

There, on the top of the house, was a fully-packed, glorious, giant-sized, sparkling, red-and-gold sleigh.

Isabel's mother looked disgusted. "Isabel—get that thing off my roof before the ceiling falls into the soup. You brought it here, you take it away."

Isabel lifted her wand.

"Oh no," said Santa. "Leave the sleigh there. But bring my reindeer here too."

Isabel was confused. "But which should I do first?" she asked.

"Sleigh," screeched her mother.

Isabel pointed her wand towards the sleigh, hoping that something—the right thing—would happen. The wand went up and down. A little smoke dribbled from the end. But nothing else appeared. Or disappeared.

Nothing at all.

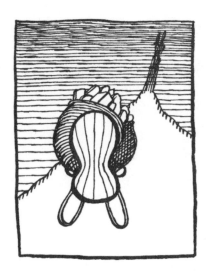 

The sleigh stayed on the roof. The reindeer stayed at the North Pole. And Santa stayed on the ground.

"I must have run out of magic," said Isabel at last.

Her mother sighed and rolled up her long black sleeves. "I should have known better. Getting rid of Santa and his sleigh takes grown-up magic. I'll have to do it myself."

She reached into her pocket, felt around a bit, and drew out a wand. It was a long wicked-looking stick. It had seventeen notches carved on the handle.

She pointed it to the North and said,

Darem, Darom, Scarem, Scalerim.

She pointed it to the South and said,

Rabid, Roachbite, Fly-by-night, Flea.

She pointed it to the East and said,

Flickering, Flackering, Fidgeting, Factual.

She pointed it towards Santa and started to say

Send him home where he ought to be . . .

when suddenly her wand, which had been long and straight, melted like a candle near a very hot fire.

"My wand, my second-best wand," screeched Isabel's mother. "What have you done to my wand?"

Santa looked unhappy. He hated to hurt anyone. Even a witch. And it was so close to midnight, he would have returned to the North Pole in any way possible—white magic, black magic. He'd even try gray. Anything so the children could have their presents for Christmas.

"This," said Isabel's mother, drawing a deep breath, "this calls for extraordinary measures." She looked significantly at Grandma.

"But I haven't tried it in years," said Grandma. "Not in hundreds of hundreds of years."

"We haven't needed it for hundreds of hundreds of years," said Isabel's mother with a quiet screech. "But we need it tonight. It's time for the MAGIC CIRCLE."

Isabel shuddered. Then she ran into the house and came out carrying a giant compass. It was as tall as Isabel, if you measured from the tips of her shoes to the top of her very tall, broad-brimmed, pointed-top, brass-buckled, very black hat. And it weighed exactly thirteen pounds.

Grandma placed one leg of the compass next to Santa.

He held on to it with a mittened hand.

The three witches pushed the other leg of the compass around. Grandma was in the lead. Isabel's mother was next. And Isabel was last, dragging her wand behind her.

Slowly a giant circle was drawn in the dirt.

"Perfect," said Grandma.

"Perfect," screeched Isabel's mother.

"Purr . . . ." said Nuncle as he watched from the stairs.

Then Grandma raised her wand. Her spell went like this:

Mmmmmm . . . brrrr . . . thesss . . . . thas . . . . .mmmmmm

Thums . . . . rimmmm . . . . bbbbllleeeee . . . shhhhhhhhh!

Or perhaps it went like this:

Arrrrhhh . . . sssshhhh . . . aannnnnnn . . . mmmmmmmmm

Crrrrrrrr . . . eeeeeee . . . . gggaaaaaa . . . hhhhhhhhhh!

Isabel couldn't be sure because it was a very secret spell that only the oldest witches knew. Besides Grandma mumbled.

Slowly, without a single sound, the circle around Santa disappeared and, in its place, was—a square.

"*That* is odd," mumbled Grandma.

"That didn't work!" screeched Isabel's mother. And she sat down on the hovel steps and began to cry. "You can't witch Santa. I can't witch Santa. And Isabel, who brought him here in the first place, can't witch Santa. If he stays here, someone is sure to find out sooner or later. And probably sooner. Oh, think of our family's reputation. Centuries of perfectly awful witches. Ruined. Ruined!"

"*Your* reputation," said Santa with a sigh. "Think of my reputation. I can't leave without someone to pull my sleigh. And if I can't leave, none of the little boys and girls will get their Christmas goodies."

"Well," said Grandma, "it's nice that *some* bad can come of this." And she sat down next to Isabel's mother. They put their heads on their hands and sighed long, terrible sighs. Santa sat down next to them, and his sighs were the loudest and longest of all.

"Maybe I should run away," Isabel whispered to Nuncle. "Maybe if I left, everything would turn out all right."

She whistled for her broom. It swept out of the house. Isabel climbed on the seat. Nuncle jumped on behind her.

"Good-bye," Isabel called as sadly as she could. She hoped that someone would ask her to stay. But they were all far too busy moaning and sighing to notice her.

The broom lifted an inch. Two inches. Finally a foot off the ground. Isabel pointed the handle tip up and started to . . .

"STOP!" shouted Santa, jumping up.

The broom stopped so suddenly, Isabel fell to the ground with a splat.

Santa came over and helped her up. "Your broom. Does it really work?"

"Most of the time," said Isabel. "Of course, it's only for learners."

"Then," said Santa, "*you* will be my reindeer."

"Oh, but I couldn't do that," Isabel said. "I'm not certain I could change into a reindeer. I might end up a dragon. Or a mouse."

Nuncle licked his mouth hungrily.

"No, no," said Santa, shaking his head. "You don't have to change into anything. Just hitch your broom to my sleigh and tow me around the world tonight."

Isabel gasped. It was a bewitching idea. She looked at her mother.

Her mother nodded. "Only go inside and dirty up first."

Her grandmother nodded. "Be sure to forget your manners."

Isabel did as she was told and then climbed back on her broom, which was pretty difficult to do since it still hovered a foot off the ground.

"Ho, ho, ho," said Isabel when she had scrambled onto the seat.

"Ho, ho, ho, yourself," said Santa, as he climbed on behind her.

And they rode up to the red-and-gold sleigh that waited on the rooftop—a sleigh that would go all around the world in a single night.

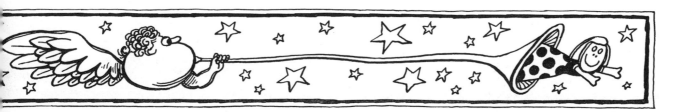

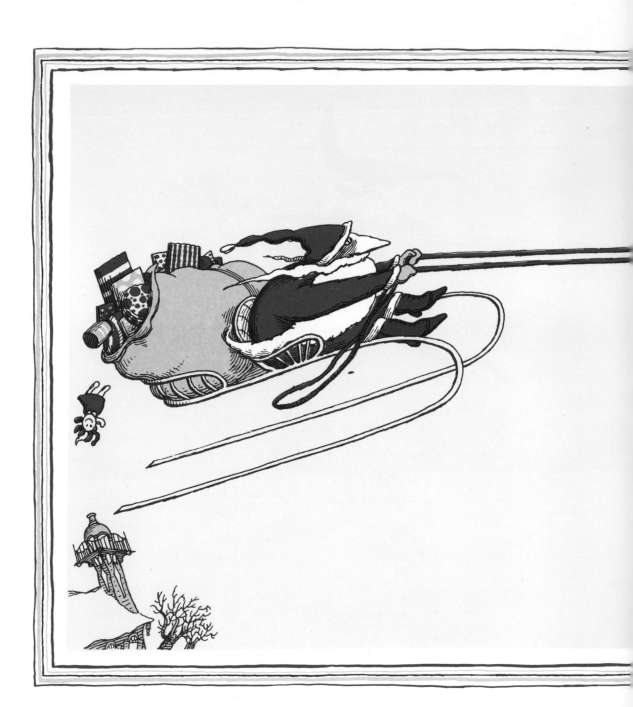

And early in the morning, when Isabel rode back from the North Pole, she had three presents packed in a basket on the back of her broom. There was a large economy-size jar of Vanishing Cream for her mother. An extra big bottle of Witch Hazel for Grandma's aches and pains. And for herself—oh, for herself—Santa had given her a bone jewelry box for her charm bracelet. And it locked with a skeleton key.